Dragons, Ogres, and Scary Things

TWO AFRICAN FOLKTALES

Dragons, Ogres, and Scary Things

TWO AFRICAN FOLKTALES

By Kathleen Arnott

Drawings by Cary

GARRARD PUBLISHING COMPANY
CHAMPAIGN, ILLINOIS

The Dragon and the Drummer Boy

One bright morning,
some girls from the village
decided to go fishing.
They got the baskets
that they used to catch fish.

They wrapped some corn bread
to take with them,
for they knew that the river
was far away.
They would have
to spend the night there.
A boy named Gatsha
watched the girls get ready.
He asked them
if he could go too.
The girls did not want
the boy to go.
Laughing, they ran away
along the narrow forest path.
But Gatsha
decided to go anyway.

When the girls
were out of sight,
he followed quietly behind.
The girls did not see him
until they reached the river.

"We told you to stay home!"
cried the girls.
"We don't want you here."
One of the girls
picked up a stick.
She shook it at Gatsha.

Then each of the girls
took her basket into the water
and began to fish.
Gatsha had no basket,
so he did not try
to join the girls.

He sat down on the bank
and watched them sadly.
While he watched,
Gatsha took out his knife.
He started to carve
the trunk of a fallen tree.
Then he cut off
the piece of wood
he had been carving.
It was about the size
of one of his father's drums.
"Since the girls
won't let me fish with them,"
he said,
"I'll make a drum for myself."
Gatsha could carve well.

Although he did not know it,
the designs he was making
on the drum were magic ones.
He worked hard all afternoon.
When the girls
came out of the river
with their fish,
he showed them the drum.
"It is very beautiful,"
they told Gatsha.
By now the sun was setting.
The girls and Gatsha
started to look
for a place
where they could
spend the night.

It was not long
before they found an empty hut.
Shouting with joy,
the girls raced inside.
Gatsha stood outside,
his magic drum under his arm.
"Come out of there," he shouted.
"I have a feeling
that it belongs
to someone evil!
Let us find another place."
The girls laughed at him
as they put their baskets
on the floor.
They made a fire outside
and cooked some of the fish.

The girls shared the fish
and the corn bread
with Gatsha.
When the moon rose,
Gatsha said
that he would play his drum
while the girls danced.
But the girls said
that they were too tired.
So they all went inside,
closed the door of the hut,
and lay down on the floor.
Soon everyone was fast asleep.
Suddenly a loud noise awoke them.
Something was growling
and roaring outside.

Gatsha peeped
through a crack
in the wall.
He saw a huge dragon
walking up and down
in the moonlight.
Gatsha was very afraid.
The dragon saw the boy.
He heard the girls' screams.
"Aha!" he roared.
"What a feast I will have.
This hut is mine,
so everything inside
is mine too!"
He pushed a large rock
against the door.

The children could not get out.

"Aha!" he roared again.

"There are many hungry animals
in the forest.

I will go and get them.

Then we can eat you up!"

The children pushed
against the door.

They could not open it.

The girls began to cry.

Gatsha told them
to stop crying.

"We must dig with our hands
at the mud wall," he said.

"We can soon
make a hole in it."

They all set to work.
At last they made
a small hole.
But just then
Gatsha heard the dragon.
He was coming
back to the hut.
"Work faster!"
he called to the girls.
"When the dragon gets here,
I will beat my drum
so he will not hear you.
When the hole is big enough,
you must climb out
one by one.
I will follow you."

By this time
the dragon was outside the hut.
He hit the rock
with one of his huge paws.
"The other animals
are on the way," he roared.

"We will soon eat you up."
Then Gatsha began to beat
his magic drum.
The dragon stopped shouting
and started to dance.
He looked very funny
as he moved back and forth,
smiling all the time.

"Work faster! Dig harder!"
whispered Gatsha.
"The dragon is dancing
but he may soon stop."
The girls worked harder
until the hole
was large enough
for the smallest girl
to get through.
At that moment
the children heard
a crashing, roaring sound
not far away.
"Work faster! Dig harder!"
cried Gatsha
as he beat on his drum.

"Here come the other animals."
Looking through the hole,
the boy saw a frightening sight.
Leopards, wild dogs, lions,
and two smaller dragons
were coming toward the hut.

The girls went on digging.
Soon they found
that the hole was big enough
for them all to climb through.
As the girls climbed out,
Gatsha beat on his drum
harder than ever.

Because the drum
was a magic one,
the sounds from it
made all the animals
start to dance.
Round and round they danced
outside the hut.

Gatsha drummed and drummed
without stopping.
The girls called to him,
"Come out! Do hurry!
We're waiting for you!"
Gatsha knew
that if he stopped drumming
the animals would stop dancing.
So, still beating his drum,
he climbed out of the hole.
Then, beating as loud
as he could,
he ran with the girls
through the forest.
At first the animals
went on dancing.

But as the children
got farther away,
the drumming became softer.
The animals
danced more and more slowly
until at last they stopped.
They were very hungry
as they stood looking at the hut.
"Let's eat the children now,"
they said to the dragon.
He moved away the big rock
and opened the door of the hut.
The animals were angry
when they found the hut empty.
"We must catch them!"
cried the dragon.

"We must catch them!"
shouted the other animals.
The animals began
to chase the children.
The children
were still running
along the forest paths
when they heard
the animals behind them.
"What shall we do?"
cried the girls.
"Get inside my magic drum,"
said Gatsha.
The girls said
that it was too small
to hold them all.

"But it's magic!"
cried the boy.
"Get inside
and you will see!"
So one by one
the girls jumped inside.
Sure enough,
it was large enough
for them all.
Then Gatsha climbed a tree,
taking the drum with him.
Just then,
the animals came racing
down the forest path.
Once again,
Gatsha began to beat his drum.

Once again,
the animals began to dance.
Gatsha went on drumming.
He was very tired,
but he knew
that he must beat his drum
until the animals
could no longer dance.

Then he saw that the animals
were getting very tired.
Soon all of them
were asleep on the ground.
Gatsha was almost too tired
to climb down the tree.
He still carried
the drum full of girls.

Quietly, he walked along
the forest path
away from the animals.
When he had gone some distance,
Gatsha opened the drum
and the girls jumped out.
"Run for your lives
before the animals wake up!"
he cried.
The children did not stop
until they reached their village.
Here they were safe,
for their fathers
were brave huntsmen.
Everyone praised Gatsha
for saving the girls' lives.

His magic drum
was given a place of honor
in the hut of the chief.
But because the people
were afraid of its magic powers,
no one ever played it again.

The Thieving Ogre

Once upon a time
a little girl named Imbali
lived in an African village.
One day her mother
got ready to go to market.
The mother said to Imbali,
"I will shut the door tightly
when I go out.

When I come back, Imbali,
I will call out your name.
Do not open the door
until you hear me call."
The mother went off to market.
Imbali was left alone
in the dark hut.
She had nothing to do.
So she lay down
on her mat bed
and sang a few songs
softly to herself.
Now Imbali did not know
that an ogre was nearby.
He had heard everything
that the mother had said.

The ogre smiled to himself.

"I will wait

a little longer.

Then I will go to the door

and call out the child's name.

When she opens the door,

I will grab her.

Then I will take her home

and eat her!"

Soon everyone in the village

had gone to the fields to work.

The ogre walked softly

to the door of Imbali's hut.

He called out

in a high voice,

"Imbali, open the door.

It is your mother."
"Why have you
come back so early?"
asked the little girl.
"You said
you would be away all day."
"Open the door,"
said the ogre,
"and I will tell you."
Imbali opened the door.
She was very frightened
when she saw the ogre.
He grabbed the little girl.
She screamed and screamed
but there was no one
in the village to hear her.

The ogre carried her
for a long time
until they reached his hut.
He put her inside
and locked the door.
"Let me out!
Let me out!" she cried.
The ogre laughed.
"I'm going to
make you fat," he said.
"Then I will let you out."
At first,
Imbali did not know
what the ogre had in mind.
He gave her
good food each day.

Then one day
some friends of the ogre
came to see him.
They looked at Imbali
through the tiny window
in the hut.
They smacked their lips.

They all agreed
that Imbali was getting fat.
"Oh, I think
they are going to eat me!"
Imbali said to herself.
"What will I do?"
She could not get away,
for the door was locked.
A large ogre
was on guard outside.
One morning
Imbali heard the ogre
talking to his friends.
"The child is fat enough
so we can eat her now.
We will have a party tonight.

Now you must help me
find a lot of firewood."
Imbali heard the footsteps
of the ogres
as they left the hut.
Even the guard
went to look for firewood.
Imbali started
to shake with fear.
"Help me! Please help me!"
she shouted loudly.
"The ogres
are going to eat me."
Just at that moment,
a small gnome-woman
was going by the hut.

She heard the cries
of the little girl.
Since she was kind and good,
she hurried toward the hut.
She unlocked the door
and picked up
the frightened child.
"Who locked you in there?"
she asked.
As they walked away,
Imbali told the gnome-woman
that the ogres
were going to eat her.
"Then I must hide you well.
Wait here
while I find what I need."

Shaking with fear,
Imbali sat under a bush.
Soon the gnome-woman came back.
She carried
a thick bamboo pole.
She put wood in one end.
"Climb into this bamboo,"
the gnome-woman told Imbali.

The gnome-woman put
another piece of wood
in the bamboo pole
to cover Imbali.
Then the clever gnome-woman
found a swarm of bees.
She got them to fly
into the top of the bamboo.
"Don't be afraid,"
she said to Imbali.
"The bees will not sting you."
Then the gnome-woman
sealed the top with wax.
She was just in time,
for as she started off,
the first of the ogres came by.

"What have you got there?"
grunted the ogre.
"Just my bees
in their new hive,"
said the gnome-woman.
"Listen and you will hear
them buzzing."

The ogre put his ear
close to the bamboo pole.
He heard the humming
of the bees.
"I don't like bees.
You can keep them,"
he said.

He went on his way.

Soon another ogre came along.

"What have you got there?"
he growled.

"Just my bees
in their new hive,"
said the gnome-woman.

"Listen and you will hear
them buzzing."

The ogre put his ear
close to the bamboo pole.

He heard the humming
of the bees.

"I don't like bees,"
he said.

"You can go on your way."

Before long, two more ogres
met the gnome-woman.
"What have you got there?"
they growled.
"Just my bees
in their new hive,"
she answered.
"Listen and you will hear
them buzzing."
After each ogre had listened,
they let the gnome-woman
go on her way.
But suddenly,
at the top of a hill,
the gnome-woman met the ogre
who had stolen Imbali.

"What are you doing
in my part of the country?"
he asked her fiercely.
"Oh, I am carrying my bees
in their hive to a new home,"
the gnome-woman said calmly.
"I don't believe you!"
growled the ogre.

"You've been stealing
from my part of the country."
"If you don't believe me,
put your ear close to the bamboo
and you will hear the buzzing!"
said the gnome-woman.
The ogre put down the firewood
he was carrying.
He listened for a minute or two.
Then he said,
"Yes, I can hear bees.
But what else
have you got in there?"
"Shall I open it up
and show you?"
asked the gnome-woman.

"Put that bamboo down
and open it up,"
growled the ogre.
"It is much too large
to hold only bees."

Carefully, the gnome-woman
put the bamboo on the ground.
She turned it
so that the top
was pointing at the ogre.

Suddenly,
she pulled out the wax
and stepped away.
Out flew the swarm of bees.
They flew right at the ogre.
They landed on his head and body.
"Help! Help!"
screamed the ogre.
He turned and ran
down the hill toward his home.
"Help! Help!
Lead me to the river!"
he shouted.
He hoped
some of his ogre friends
would come to help.

After he had gone,
the gnome-woman
picked up the bamboo
and hurried off
toward Imbali's village.
She told Imbali
not to be afraid.
"We will soon
reach your village,"
the gnome-woman said.
"Then I will let you out
of the bamboo."
The sun was setting
as the gnome-woman
walked into Imbali's village.
"Come here, everyone!" she cried.

"I have brought you a present."
The people were not afraid
of the gnome-woman.
They gathered around her
and the bamboo she carried.
Among the people
was Imbali's mother.
Her eyes were red from crying,
for she thought
that she would never see
her child again.
Carefully,
the gnome-woman
took out the piece of wax.
"Come out! Come out!"
cried the gnome-woman.

Imbali climbed out of the bamboo.
She stood smiling
at all the villagers.
"Imbali!" they cried.
"We thought
we would never see you again!"
"Mother!" shouted Imbali
as she ran to her.
They hugged each other.
"The gnome-woman
saved me from the ogres,"
she said.
"They were going
to eat me tonight!"
Everyone was very glad
to have Imbali home again.

A feast was held that night.
The gnome-woman
sat in the place of honor.
She was given
all the best food to eat.

When midnight came
the gnome-woman said
that she must leave.
Away she went,
followed by the thanks
of all the villagers.
Imbali wanted very much
to meet the gnome-woman again.
But she never saw her.
She never saw the ogres either.
When she was grown
and had children of her own,
she often told them the story.
She told them
how the kind gnome-woman
had saved her life.